Where the Gardens Grow

A story about sharing kindness

Written by Nicoline Evans   Illustrated by Elise Hollandsworth Hartmann

There once was a princess with the most beautiful garden. It spanned the fields surrounding her kingdom, and grew bright for all to see.

Beyond the castle gates, the
world was dusty and barren. With
no seeds for the people to plant,
flowers never grew there.

All types of flowers grew in the castle garden,
but her favorite were the kindness flowers.
    Whenever she had a bad day, she went to her garden
and sat amongst her kindness flowers, letting their beauty
remind her that tomorrow would be a better day.

The flowers were kind—they were gentle, they brought her joy, and they made her feel safe.

Afraid that others might hurt them, no one was allowed to touch these flowers except her, and she guarded them with a fierce heart.

"Darling, why do you look so sad?" the queen mother asked one rainy afternoon.

"I am stuck inside and I don't have anyone to play with," the princess answered.

"Invite one of your friends over," her mother said. "Everyone is welcome here."

The princess replied, "The flowers are my friends, and they can't come inside."

"While it is wonderful that you find comfort amongst the flowers, it is important to make friends with the children here, too."

The princess was conflicted. She still worried that the other children might not treat her garden with kindness.

The sun returned the following day, and the princess continued to protect her lavish garden. She shooed away the children who often stopped their games to stare at her glorious field of flowers.

"They are lovely," the little girl who lived in the kingdom next door shouted.

"They are mine," the princess replied.

"Can I sit with you?" her neighbor asked.

"In my garden?"

"Yes."

"No one is allowed in here except me," the princess declared.

"That's a shame," the little girl replied. "Kindness is meant to be shared."

The little girl walked away, leaving the princess baffled. *Was I unkind to my neighbor?* the princess wondered. She looked at the beauty all around her, then beyond the golden gates where the land was stark and colorless.

Inside the castle, she spoke to her mother.

"Why are there no flowers beyond our castle gates?" the princess asked.

Her mother answered, "The flowers spread when kindness is shared."

The princess thought of the little girl she had shooed away.

"Is sharing kindness a way to make friends, too?" she asked.

"Of course!" her mother confirmed.

The princess bowed her head in shame. "While protecting my flowers, I was unkind to someone who could have been a friend."

"You must find a way to make it right," the queen advised. "Sometimes kindness must be learned."

Aware now that she had made a terrible mistake, the princess went to bed with a heavy heart.

The sun rose the next morning, and from her window, her colorful garden glowed in its light. Determined to correct her error, she came up with an idea.

She raced into the field and found the most perfect kindness flower. With a gentle touch, she removed one of its many seeds from the center of its blossom.

She walked to the edge of her garden and waited by the golden gate. Morning turned into afternoon before she saw her neighbor again.

"Hey!" the princess shouted as the little girl crossed a dusty path on her way home. "Can I show you something?"

The little girl narrowed her brow in curiosity and changed direction, walking toward the princess's lush garden instead.

"I want to give this to you," the princess revealed. The kindness seed sat in the center of her palm.

"What is it?" the little girl asked.

"A flower seed. Now you can have a garden just like mine."

The little girl's eyes lit up with excitement.
"Thank you!" she exclaimed, carefully holding the seed
to her heart. "Maybe tomorrow you can help me plant it."
The princess smiled. "I would love to help."

From that day forward, the two little girls became the best of friends. They helped each other care for their ever-growing gardens, and shared their plentiful abundance of kindness seeds with everyone in the land.

"I am proud of you," the queen mother professed, kissing the princess's forehead. "Like one of your flowers, you have blossomed with kindness. Look at the beauty you've created."

The princess looked out the window of the castle tower to discover that the landscape had changed.

One tiny seed of kindness spread beauty across the entire land, and the colorful flowers brought happiness to all.

The world was a better
place where kindness was
allowed to grow.

Where the Gardens Grow

ISBN: 978-1-7345660-4-8
Printed in the United States of America

Learn more about the Author and Illustrator!

Author - Nicoline Evans

www.nicolineevans.com
Amazon: www.amazon.com/author/nicolineevans
Facebook: www.facebook.com/nicolinenovels
Instagram: www.instagram.com/nicolinenovels
Twitter: www.twitter.com/nicolinenovels

Illustrator - Elise Hollandsworth Hartmann

www.thedarkfaerie.com
Facebook: www.facebook.com/darkfaeriecreations
Instagram: www.instagram.com/thedarkfaerie
Pinterest: www.pinterest.com/darkfaerie

Made in the USA
Middletown, DE
27 October 2021